TRICYCLE
and
Friends

True-Life Adventures of a Three-Legged Golden Retriever and His Rescued Farm Animal Friends

Lester Aradi

Archway Publishing books may be ordered through booksellers or by contacting:

Archway Publishing
1663 Liberty Drive
Bloomington, IN 47403
www.archwaypublishing.com
1 (888) 242-5904

ISBN: 978-1-4808-4205-2 (sc)
ISBN: 978-1-4808-4206-9 (hc)
ISBN: 978-1-4808-4207-6 (e)

Print information available on the last page.

Archway Publishing rev. date: 01/13/2017

DEDICATION

To my incredible wife Diane for your vision in creating a small farm animal sanctuary for adopted rescued animals; as well as your support and encouragement to put our beautiful life's mission into this story. Your hard work and love for all of us made this possible.

ACKNOWLEDGMENTS

Without the help and support of the following people and organizations our rescued animals and this book would not be possible.

Lee Roesner of Paradigm Graphic Design for the front cover layout and design. www.paradigmgraphic.com

Renea Winchester for your editorial assistance.

To the great staff of Archway Publishing for all your support in guiding us though our first effort of self publication.

Adopt a Golden Atlanta for adopting Tricycle and Romeo to us.

Golden Retriever Rescue Atlanta for adopting us Sampson, now living across the Rainbow Bridge.

Union County Georgia Animal Control for asking us to foster and then adopting Major to us. Now also living across the Rainbow Bridge.

Hope Equine Rescue in Auburndale, Florida for starting us on this journey by adopting our first rescued horse, Haggis Hanover, to us.

The Georgia Equine Rescue League for entrusting us with foster horses and also adopting them to us.

To the South East Llama Rescue for both foster and adopted llamas and alpacas.

To our wonderful community and friends in Blue Ridge, Georgia.

Lastly, to all the guests of our small business, Horse Creek Stable Bed and Breakfast, from which all proceeds go to the care and feeding of our animals. You make this happen.

AUTHOR'S NOTE

Tricycle is a real life rescued three legged Golden Retriever. He, along with his other rescued animal friends, live at Horse Creek Stable Bed and Breakfast in the North Georgia Mountains, just outside Blue Ridge, Georgia.

Visitors are always welcome. Children with special needs are especially welcome.

Follow Tricycle and his friends at:
https://www.facebook.com/tricycleandfriends
www.horsecreekstable.com

"Tricycle"

CHAPTER ONE

. . . .

**Tricycle, a rescued three legged Golden Retriever, arrives at his
new home and is greeted by Buckaroo, a miniature donkey.**

"Hi, my name is Tricycle. I'm a Golden Retriever. Are you a dog?" asks Tricycle.

"No, I'm a miniature donkey. My name is Buckaroo. You must be new here," says Buckaroo.

"Yes, I was just adopted. Today is my first day," replies Tricycle.

"What does adopted mean?" asks Buckaroo.

"Adopted means that I am very special. I needed a new home and people that love me very much brought me home to live with them and be part of their family," explains Tricycle.

"Hey, I see that you only have three legs. What happened to you?" asks Buckaroo.

"I was hit by a car and broke my leg very badly. The animal doctors had to remove it," said Tricycle.

"Did it hurt?" asked Buckaroo.

Tricycle replied, "It did when it happened, but it doesn't anymore."

Buckaroo asks, "Does it slow you down?"

"Not at all," replies Tricycle. "I can run as fast as any other dog."

"Do you want to race?" asks Buckaroo.

"Sure. Bet I can beat ya," said Tricycle.

Both Tricycle and Buckaroo begin to race around the barn.

When they finish, Tricycle proudly boasts "See, I told you I can run fast. I beat you."

"That was fast," agrees Buckaroo. "But can you jump?"

Tricycle replies, "I sure can. I jumped right up into the car when my new human parents picked me up."

"I'm very impressed," says Buckaroo. "You are very brave."

Tricycle smiles and says, "Thanks. When I make up my mind, I can do anything."

"Don't you miss your leg?" asks Buckaroo.

"I do sometimes, but I decided that I can do as much as I want to do without it," said Tricycle. "Are there other animals here on this farm?" asks Tricycle.

"Oh yes," replies Buckaroo. "A lot of other animals live here. We have horses, llamas, alpacas, other dogs, chickens and even honey bees."

Tricycle asks, "Are they adopted just like me?"

"Most of them are. We are one big happy family with human parents who love us very much," said Buckaroo.

"Will you take me to meet them?" begs Tricycle.

"Sure, but I'm a little hungry," replies Buckaroo. "Let's go after lunch. Sit with me while I eat."

"What are you eating?" asks Tricycle.

"It's called hay. It's tall grass that is cut just for us," said Buckaroo. "That's what horses and donkeys eat. You can say we are vegetarians. No meat for us."

"No meat!" exclaimed Tricycle. "That wouldn't be my choice. Give me a steak bone any day."

"That was yummy," said Buckaroo with a full tummy. "I'll get my good friend Emma to walk us down to meet the llamas."

Buckaroo introduces Tricycle to the other animals. "Tricycle, meet Cantara and Pink. These are the llamas I was telling you about. They needed a new home so they came here."

"Glad to meet you both. My name is Tricycle."

"Glad to meet you too," replies Cantara.

Pink, the other llama, asks "Are you a friendly dog?"

"I'm very friendly. I love everybody. Especially little children," said Tricycle.

"Be careful Tricycle, they like to spit," warns Buckaroo.

"We do not. We never spit at people or dogs . . . only donkeys that try to eat our food," said Pink, giving Buckaroo a dirty look.

"It was only one time," replies Buckaroo, lowering his head.

"Can you do tricks, like sit or go fetch like a dog?" asks Tricycle.

Cantara says, " No, but we love to go hiking in the woods very much. We have a very important job. We carry backpacks for people while they hike. Maybe one day you would like to join us. Can you go for long walks with only three legs?"

"I sure can, I just need to stop and rest once in a while," Tricycle said proudly.

"Let's go now. I need some exercise," offers Cantara.

After their walk Pinks says, "You kept up pretty good for a dog with only three legs."

"I told you that I could. What else do you do?" asks Tricycle.

"We grow our hair out really long in the winter and then when summer rolls around our owners cut it off," replies Pink. "Just like going to a barber."

"What do they do with it?" asks Tricycle.

"They sell it to other people who use it to knit scarfs and sweaters; but our owners give small amounts to kids who are sick and need good luck getting better. They call it Llama Love Luck," said Cantara.

"That is nice. I heard our owners say that they wanted sick kids to come visit me too," said Tricycle with a smile.

"We have to go back now Tricycle, it's getting later," warns Buckaroo.

"Will you come back tomorrow?" asks Cantara. "I heard our parents say that it will be a special day. A five day old alpaca is coming. His mother needs help feeding him so we get to help take care of him for her," smiles Cantara.

"Will children get to feed him with a bottle just like a baby?" asks Tricycle.

"You bet," says Pink. "See you tomorrow."

"Goodbye. I'll be back for more fun," says Tricycle as he heads back to the house. "See you tomorrow."

Tricycle with his horse friend Atlas

Buckaroo with his very special friend

Tricycle spending time with his horses

A young friend bottle feeding Bakari

CHAPTER TWO

. . . .

"Buckaroo, hey Buckaroo, wake up," shouts Tricycle.

"Go away Tricycle I'm not ready to get up yet," said Buckaroo, still yawning.

"You have to get up. Our new baby brother just got here. He looks nothing like us," said Tricycle.

"Of course he doesn't. He is an alpaca that our parents just adopted," replies Buckaroo.

"He is so small. I just want to lick his face to show that I love him," said Tricycle.

"What does adopted mean again?" asks Buckaroo.

"Sometimes an animal's parents can't take really good care of them, even though they love them very much," explains Tricycle. "So a new family that has a lot of love to give will bring them home and love them with all their hearts."

"We are lucky that everybody loves us so much," replies Buckaroo.

"He looks just like the llamas, only smaller," said Tricycle.

"That's because llamas and alpacas are very similar animals, just like donkeys and horses," explains Buckaroo.

Tricycle says in a soft voice "Shhhh, they are coming this way. I think that our new brother is going to stay here in the barn with you and one of the older alpacas, Bourbon."

"I heard that the baby alpaca was very small and sick when he was born so his mommy needed us to help teach him how to drink milk from a baby bottle," said Buckaroo.

"Buckaroo, you never told me why you came here," inquires Tricycle.

"When I was little, the bigger donkeys would always bully me," said Buckaroo.

"What does bully mean?" asks Tricycle.

"That's when other animals pick on you. It's not very kind," replies Buckaroo.

"I don't like bullies," said Tricycle.

"Nobody likes bullies because they are not nice. They say and do hurtful things on purpose. Good animals are always very nice to each other," said Buckaroo.

Tricycle eagerly says "Wait, here they come." "Excuse me Bourbon, but can you introduce our new brother to us?" asks Tricycle.

"Yes," said Bourbon. "Buckaroo and Tricycle, meet Bakari. Bakari, this is Buckaroo the miniature donkey, and Tricycle the three legged Golden Retriever."

"Hello friends, I'm happy to meet you," said baby Bakari.

"Why do they call you Bakari?" asks Tricycle.

Bakari says, "It's an African word that means hopeful. I was so sick when I was born that everybody was hopeful I would get better."

"Are you better now?" asks Buckaroo.

"Oh yes, I am much better, thank you," replies Bakari.

"Good, that makes us happy," said Tricycle.

"Bakari, look. I see some children coming this way with a baby bottle full of milk. I bet the bottle they are carrying is for you," said Buckaroo.

"See you later, I'm hungry," said Bakari.

Tricycle and Buckaroo smile at one another because Bakari is so cute and nice.

"Let's go up to the house Buckaroo. I want you to meet another dog named Major. You will like him," said Tricycle.

"I met him a few years ago when he came here," said Buckaroo.

"He told me that he was very old and very tired and that he was ready to cross the Rainbow Bridge," said Tricycle.

"What's a Rainbow Bridge?" asks Buckaroo.

"It is like heaven. It's where all the animals go and where they wait until their humans go to heaven. They go there and greet all the people that were kind to them. It's a very happy and peaceful place for animals," explains Tricycle.

"That's very nice. Let's race up to the house and tell Major that we love him," said Buckaroo.

Young boy with a cast visiting Romeo

Buckaroo counting Romeo's legs

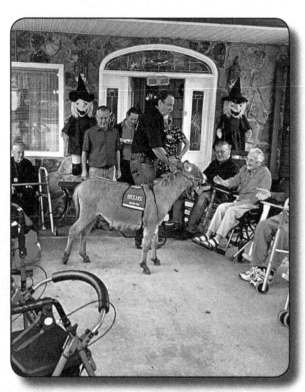

**Buckaroo visiting with
very special friends**

Telling Major how much we love him

CHAPTER THREE

....

"Buckaroo, Buckaroo, our parents are very sad. I'm sad too," cried Tricycle.

"What's wrong?" asked Buckaroo.

"Major passed away and crossed over the Rainbow Bridge this afternoon," said Tricycle.

"Don't be too sad. Major lived here on the farm for the last three years. It was the best years of his life. He was very happy here," replied Buckaroo.

"I know. He got to run free and was loved very much by everybody," Tricycle said.

"Did our parents bury him up on the hill so Major can look down on the rest of us all the time?" asked Buckaroo.

"They did and they put a beautiful plant on his grave," said Tricycle.

"That's very special. His spirit will always be on the farm," Buckaroo said.

"Guess what Major said to our parents just before he left?" Tricycle asked.

"What did he say?" Buckaroo asked.

"He said to everybody, 'Don't be too sad. I love you very much and I know that you love me too. I had a very happy life thanks to all your kindness,' " Tricycle told Buckaroo.

"Did he say anything else?" asked Buckaroo.

"He did. He said, 'I want you to show how much you love me by adopting another rescued dog that needs a home, and love him or her as much as you love all of us,' " Tricycle said.

"That's a hard thing to do right away; but it is a nice way to honor Major," Buckaroo said. "I know what this means. We will be getting another dog soon."

"I hope so. Adopting another rescued dog is a good thing. I'm excited to see who our new brother or sister will be. I'll see you later," said Tricycle. "I have to go. Our parents are calling."

One Week Later

"Buckaroo, come meet our new brother," Tricycle said.

"Hi, I'm Buckaroo. What's your name?"

"Hi, my name is Romeo. I'm a Golden Retriever."

"I'm very happy to meet you. Welcome to our farm. Where did you come from?" asked Buckaroo.

"I came from a dog rescue group called Adopt A Golden in Atlanta," said Romeo.

"Buckaroo, look closer. Do you see what Romeo and I have in common?" asked Tricycle.

"Oh my gosh, I just noticed. You only have three legs, just like Tricycle," said Buckaroo. "And you are both missing the same leg!"

"That's right," said Romeo.

"How did you lose your leg?" asked Buckaroo.

"I lost it the same way that Tricycle lost his. I was hit by a car. I didn't listen to other people who kept telling me not to run into the street," said Romeo.

"It's always important to listen to your parents and teachers," said Buckaroo.

"I know, I learned that the hard way," agreed Romeo.

"Can you run as fast as Tricycle?" asked Buckaroo.

"I can do anything that I make up my mind to do. Nothing can slow me down," said Romeo.

"Buckaroo, Romeo said that he wants children to come to our farm and visit. Especially children that lost a leg or have trouble walking themselves," said Tricycle.

"What a great idea!" agreed Buckaroo. "I love visitors."

"I'm glad you said that because we are going somewhere very special tomorrow," said Tricycle. "All three of us."

"Where is that, Tricycle?" asked Buckaroo.

"All three of us are going to a place where old people live. We get to cheer everybody up," said Tricycle.

"Hee haw, I love doing that," said Buckaroo. "I love people of all ages."

"I can't wait to meet all the nice people," said Tricycle. "They always scratch my tummy."

"Good, I'm excited," said Buckaroo.

"Goodbye Buckaroo. We need to take a bath so we look good for tomorrow," said Romeo. "See you bright and early."

Watch for more books and stories about the real life animals of "Tricycle and Friends."

CPSIA information can be obtained
at www.ICGtesting.com
Printed in the USA
LVOW06s1035060217
523340LV00027B/420/P